Bing Bang Boogie, it's a Boy Scout

Bob Wilson

Collins

Look out for more *Jets* from Collins

Jessy Runs Away • *Best Friends* • **Rachel Anderson**
Ivana the Inventor • *Ernest the Heroic Lion Tamer* • **Damon Burnard**
Two Hoots • *Almost Goodbye Guzzler* • **Helen Cresswell**
Shadows on the Barn • **Sara Garland**
Nora Bone • *The Mystery of Lydia Dustbin's Diamonds* • **Brough Girling**
Thing on Two Legs • *Thing in a Box* • **Diana Hendry**
Desperate for a Dog • *More Dog Trouble* • **Rose Impey**
Georgie and the Dragon • *Georgie and the Planet Raider* • **Julia Jarman**
Cowardy Cowardy Cutlass • *Free With Every Pack* • **Robin Kingsland**
Mossop's Last Chance • *Mum's the Word* • **Michael Morpurgo**
Hiccup Harry • *Harry Moves House* • **Chris Powling**
Rattle and Hum, Robot Detectives • *Rattle and Hum in Double Trouble* • **Frank Rodgers**
Our Toilet's Haunted • **John Talbot**
Rhyming Russell • *Messages* • **Pat Thomson**
Monty the Dog Who Wears Glasses • *Monty's Ups and Downs* • **Colin West**
Ging Gang Goolie, it's an Alien • *Stone the Crows, it's a Vacuum Cleaner* • **Bob Wilson**

For Matilda, Reuben and Babik

First published by A & C Black Ltd in 1997
Published by Collins in 1998
10 9 8 7 6 5
Collins is an imprint of HarperCollins*Publishers*Ltd,
77–85 Fulham Palace Road, Hammersmith, London W6 8JB

ISBN 0 00 675313 2

A CIP record for this title is available from the British Library.

Printed in Great Britain by
Clays Ltd, St Ives plc

Way out in space millions of billions of squillions of miles away from the small planet we call Earth, there is an even smaller planet called GROB.

On this planet live a race of alien space monsters called –

THE GROBBLEWOCKIANS.

Once upon a time, back in the 1980s the Grobblewockians were said to be . . .

But not any more.

Things are different now.

Nowadays Grobblewockians have a reputation for being honest, peaceful, law-abiding citizens who spend most of their time thinking of others – and making up names for knots.

Indeed, it's now often said that the average Grobblewockian is so timid *he wouldn't even say 'Boo!' to a goose.*

What brought about this change?

Historians of the future might claim:

A That saintly beings of high spiritual intelligence taught the Grobblewockians the error of their ways.

Or maybe historians might claim:

B That the Grobblewockians were put in the care of well-meaning, but power-crazed, dictators who taught them about truth, justice, the dire consequences of anti-social behaviour, and how an oxbow lake is formed.

But the historians will be wrong.

Because the truth is:

C They gave up being evil because they discovered that...

1. Conquering planets
2. Destroying civilisations
3. Pillaging
4. Looting
5. Murdering innocent bystanders and
6. Vandalising bus shelters

was not half as much fun as 

being in

SCOWTS

BEE PREE
PEAR HEAD

A note from THE AUTHOR

You're probably thinking –
"I don't believe this. People don't
change from being horrid
monsters one minute to
happy Scouts the next!
What happened?"

Well, what happened was this...
In 1988 a Grobblewockian called GROTT
came down to Earth in a Scout Ship
and landed in the middle of a Boy Scout Camp.
He wasn't a particularly evil alien – but he
did have a Mega Powerful Laser Ray-Gun
and would have blown the
head off this particular
Boy Scout. But...

...but that's
another story.

No, I mean it really is another story.
It's a 'JETS' story called...
"Ging Gang Goolie, It's an Alien"
Now this particular Boy Scout's
name was ⇒ GARRY WIMBUSH

It was Garry Wimbush
who taught Grott about
Scouting, and how to
Speak English – and
you need to know this
because...
he's in this story too.

But this story takes place 64 years later.
The Year is 2052.

AND NOW

THIS IS GARRY WIMBUSH.

He is a grandad.

And, along with the rest of the old 3rd Balsawood Road Scout troop he lives in . . .

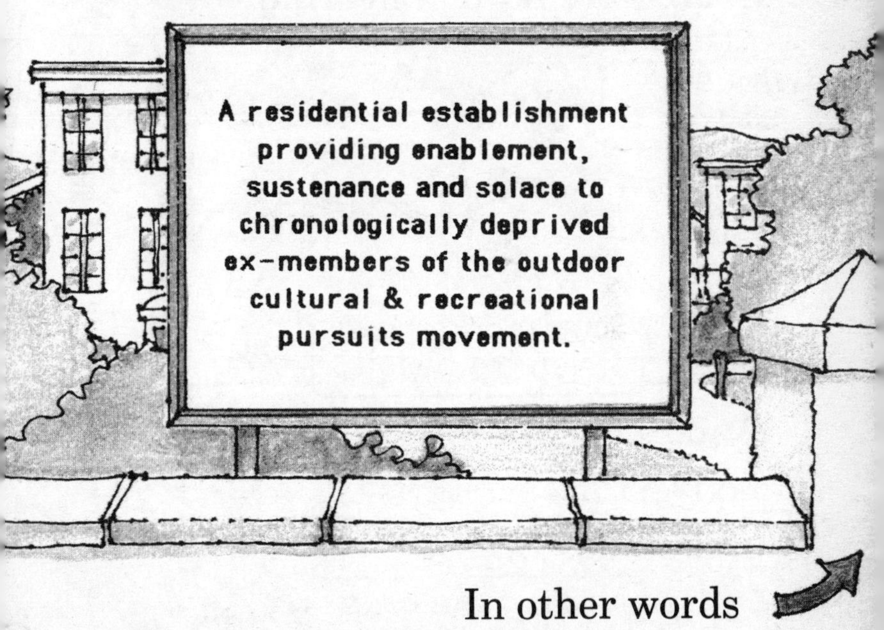

In other words

Some of the old scouts were now short-sighted.

Some were hard of hearing.

And Skip (who was 92), had lost his sense of direction.

But their hearts were strong,
their minds were clear,
and their memories stretched right
back to the good old days.

He was a million, billion, squillion miles away, on the planet GROB. And he too was talking about the past.

Grott was very proud of his grandson. For Gribble was a good scout, and had earned . . .

There was however, one badge he didn't have, one test that he had failed to pass.
It was:

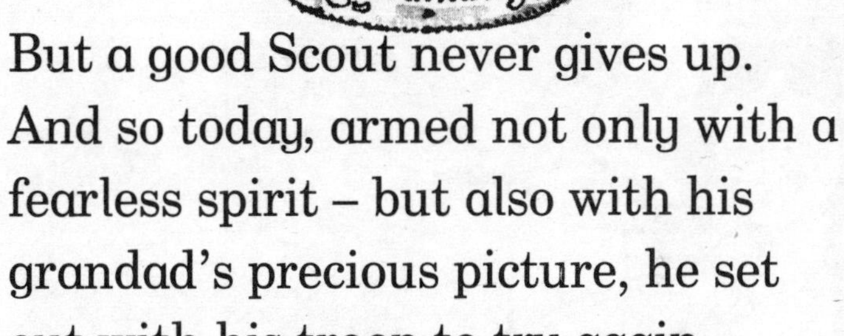

But a good Scout never gives up. And so today, armed not only with a fearless spirit – but also with his grandad's precious picture, he set out with his troop to try again.

Grandad Wimbush had a grandson too. His name was . . .

DIMBERT

Today Dimbert was going to visit his grandad. His mother said it might do him some good.

said his mother.

So he did.

He talked about why he needed a modem upgrade, the disadvantages of RAM doubling on a PC 6500 – and how Squark 7.5B wasn't compatible with an IBM running at 1280Mhz. Then he said:

Grandad Wimbush listened to all this very carefully, thought about it for a moment – and then said:

Now when I tell you that only that morning Dimbert had . . .

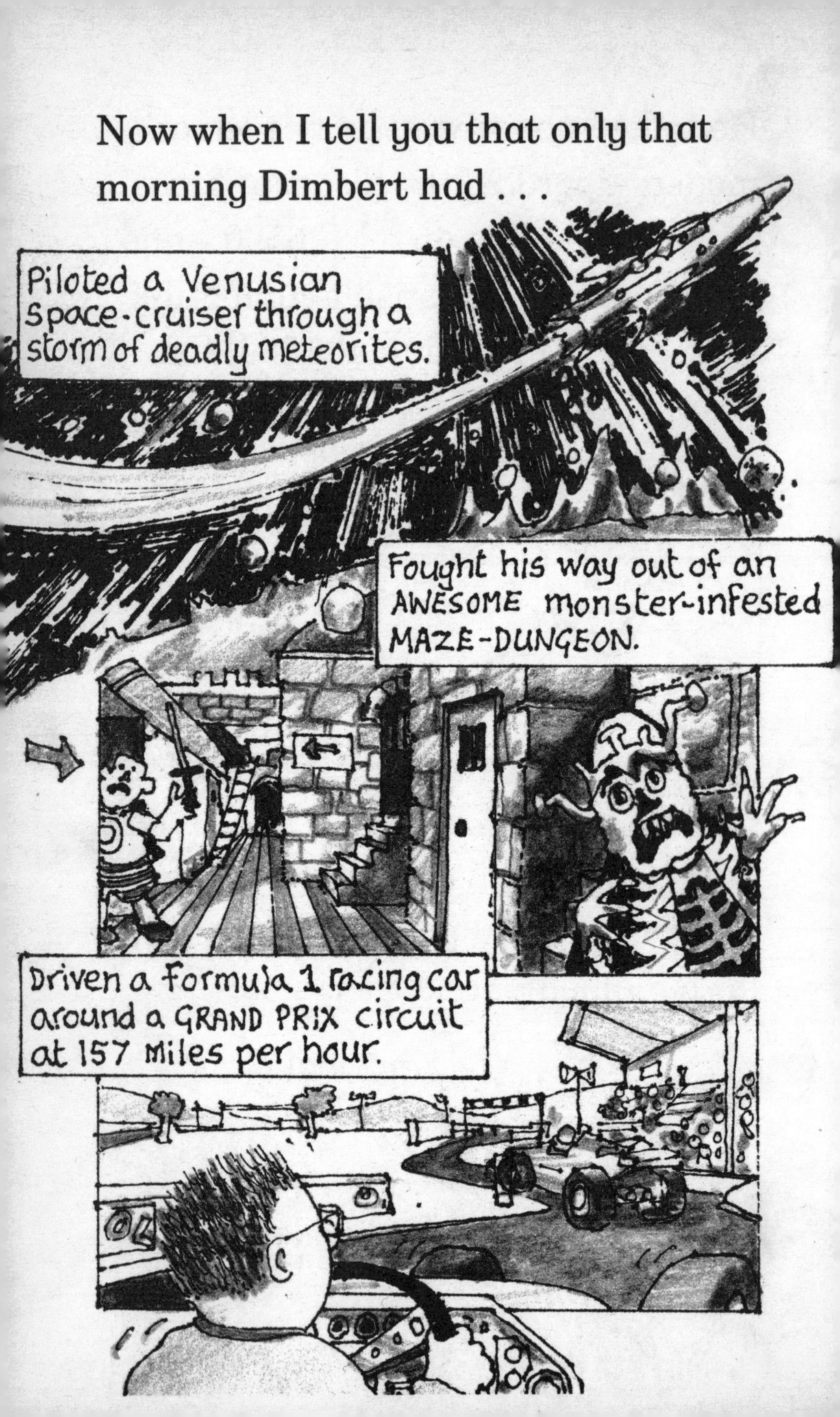

And then played Megaball, Hypercop, and Super-Mega-hyper BLAST-O-CRICKET, (amassing a total score of 17,568 not out).

. . . you might wonder what he was so fed up about. And like Grandad Wimbush, you might wonder what he was talking about.

'He's talking about computers,' said the tea lady. 'It's computer talk.' Grandad didn't understand computer talk. He thought:

That a **PC** was somebody who went around arresting burglars.

That **RAM** was a male sheep.

That **Software** was what you went to bed in.

That a **Cursor** was someone who swore a lot.

And that **Dot Matrix** was the name of the tea lady.

The name of the tea lady was not Dot Matrix, but she did have a son who was into computers, and so she was able to translate.

exclaimed Grandad Wimbush.

But it's not raining! It's a lovely misty, moisty Autumn day. If I was your age I wouldn't be bored. On a day like today I'd be out and about. I'd be up the park or down the woods collecting conkers with my mates.

A NOTE FROM THE AUTHOR.

You may think it odd that Dimbert knew nothing about CONKERS. But you must remember that this story is set in THE FUTURE. And in 2052 Conkers will be just one of the things that children won't know about any more. They will also not know about:

skateboards

swings

kites

Catapults

frisbees

Yo-Yos

buckets and spades

sledges

Skipping ropes or marbles.

So what **will** they know about?

Computers.

Dimbert loved his computer.

. . . on the planet GROB,

Gribble and the Grobblewockian

Scouts had a much bigger problem.

They had failed the badge yet again.

Now, to earn the Backwoodsman badge you need to have: determination, stamina, fortitude, know-how, resourcefulness and pluck.

You also need to have . . . **a wood.**

And that was the problem; GROB was a totally treeless planet.

Gribble and his troop had hiked the length and breadth of it but all they had ever found were . . .

stumps!

According to Grandad Grott, there had once been lots of trees. But Orrice Dee-orrible, the most evil of all the 'old-style' Grobblewockians, had blasted them all to smithereens while testing his terrible invention.

'What shall we do?' asked Gribble.

Meanwhile...

On a funny little planet called Earth, Dimbert was waiting for a train. He was going home on the **C**omputer-**R**egulated, **A**uto-**I**ntelligent, **Z**one-**I**ntegrated **T**rain **S**ystem – known for short as:

These trains had no driver; they were entirely computer controlled. At first people had worried about this. But scientific experts had assured them.

And politicians had reassured them.

Not all that far out in SPACE...
alien scouts were
heading towards Earth.
Just now they were passing by
a small planet called 'Oink',
and playing I-spy.
I-spy with my bulging eye something beginning with - P.
Peg?
Plug?

Gribble wasn't playing I-spy; he was poking around under his seat. He hoped to find something to play with . . . and he did.

For under the seat he found –

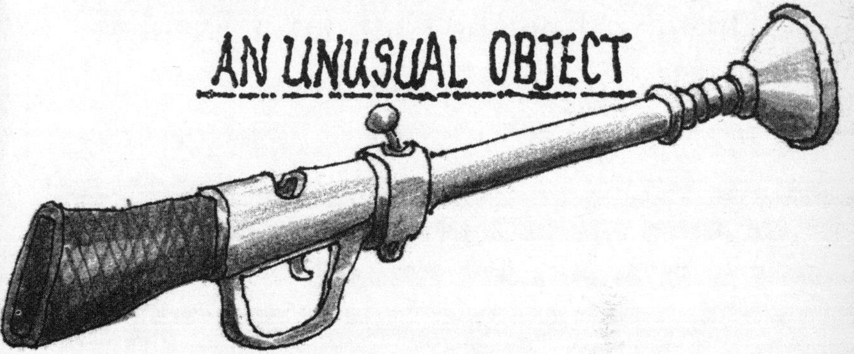

'Gosh,' he thought, 'this antique object looks like it might be one of those horribly powerful, lazy-gun zappy things that Grandad Grott was telling us about.'

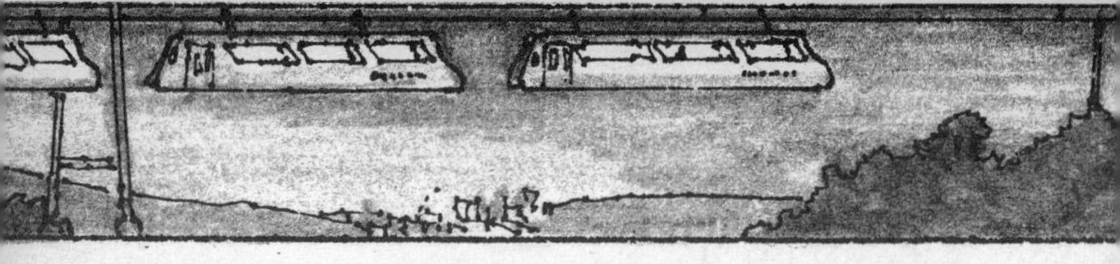

Meanwhile, Dimbert was on the train. There was nothing much to see out of the window – just trees and stuff. He consulted the Computer Display Screen to see where he was.

It said:

We are passing over the arboreal conservation area formerly known as Black...bank Woo....oo!!

Suddenly . . . there was a blinding flash of laser-white light and the sign said:

LAZERRRR

OOh!!

ZAP!!!

ARghh!!

There was a pause. Then it said:

Erh........ sorry about that...where was I?..
...Oh yes....ALL PASsENGERS ALIGHT HERE..

Dimbert, obedient to the computer's instructions, stepped out of the door.

Had he glanced back at the sign he would have seen that it now said:

....Oh... yes......I forgot to mention....Erh..
PLEASE MIND THE STEP......

But he didn't glance back at the sign. He was too busy hurtling head over heels down into the darkness.

He landed, unharmed, but in a strange and alien place. Even if he could have seen where he was he wouldn't have known where he was. He'd never been in a wood before.

For a brief moment
the sky was illuminated by
a streak of light, not unlike a
falling shooting star.

Then the spooky darkness
folded around him once more.
And he was scared.
He decided to wait until the street lamps came on before he made a move.

And so he waited.

But the street lamps didn't come on.

It just got darker.

He was wondering what on earth he could do when . . .
he noticed a flickering light in the distance.

Civilisation!

he thought,

and started blundering towards it **but**
he was stopped in his tracks by

a terrible BLOOD CURDLING WAIL!!

It was the Grobblewockian Scouts singing . . .

Bing-BANG...
Boogie-Boogie-Boogie.

* Bing-BANG.

oogie-Boogie
TCH-STRAP!
Bing-Bang-Boo!

A NOTE From: THE AUTHOR
You may be thinking -
They're singing the WRONG WORDS
It should be - "Ging Gang Goolie"
not - "Bing Bang Boogie".
But you're forgetting
something.

You're forgetting that this story is set IN THE FUTURE. People change with the times and as people change the sort of words that they use change too.
For example:-

In the 16th century, minstrels travelled the length and breadth of the land. They sang ditties and ballads, and love songs with words like:

These words probably sounded to you like *a load of meaningless twaddle*. And no wonder; they are 16th-century words.
Things are different now.

We still have minstrels of a sort. And they still go on nationwide tours. We call them pop singers. But how their songs have changed. For their songs reflect the world of fast-moving information technology in which we live. They have words designed to be instantly understood. Words like –

To a 16th-century minstrel these words would sound like *a load of meaningless drivel.*

Odd that isn't it?

This story is set in a future time.
It's 64 years since the Grobblewockians attempted to conquer Earth.
In the course of time the names of things and places often get changed. Especially by people (or aliens) who are doing a spot of conquering.
FOR EXAMPLE :–

You probably know the capital city of England as:

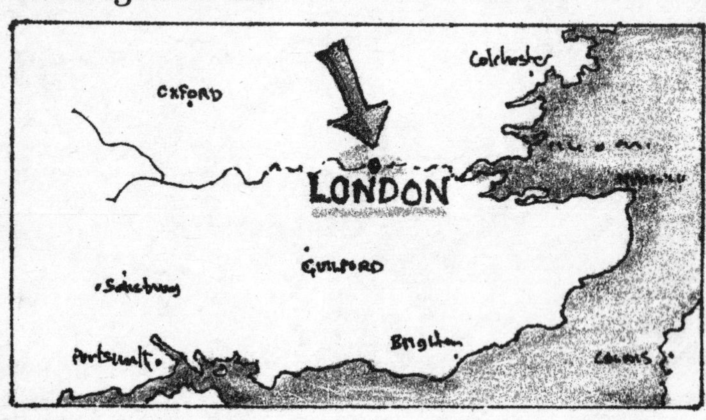

But the place we now call London the Ancient Romans called:

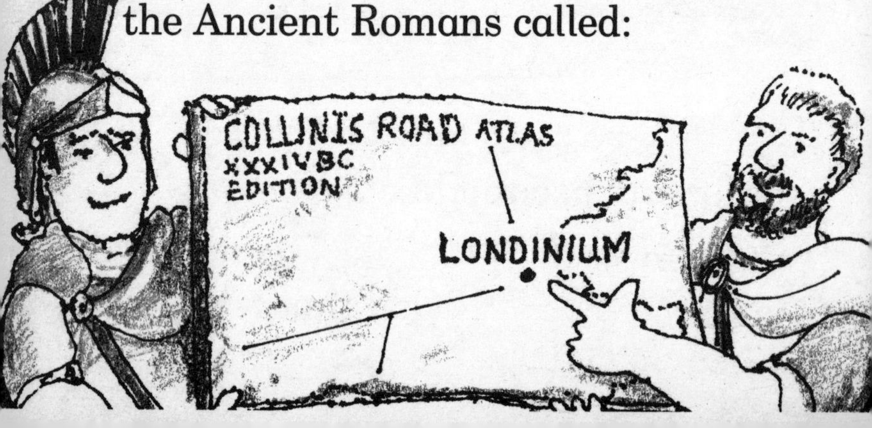

So had Dimbert been walking along the banks of the river Tamesis in 54BC he might have chanced upon a troop of Roman soldiers sitting around a camp fire scoffing oysters and singing:

LONDIN-I-UM'S BRIDGE...
IS NOT YET BUILT
Not yet built... not yet built...

One last example:

STONE AGE CAVE PEOPLE

In prehistoric times most things hadn't been discovered yet. And people then had so few words they probably weren't sure what to call the things they *had* got.

Can you imagine what Dimbert might have heard if he'd stumbled across some Stone Age cave men having a sing song?

Oh...we ain't got a barr-el of
May-be we're.....
Erhh?
Uhmm?
But we go like this

!?
Erhh?
doing...what we're doing now.
side by side.

Back in 1988
Garry Wimbush had told Grott all about Scouting.
Grott had then told other Grobblewockians what
he'd been told. - and they told other aliens
what they'd been told. And so the Word spread.
But alien memories are unreliable and words
get misheard and repeated wrongly.

FOR EXAMPLE:-
Garry told Grott → A Scout smiles and whistles under all difficulties.

But Grott told the others → A Scout mildly whispers under all difficulties.

By 2052 it was being said that → A Scout likes highland drizzle and adores difficult trees.

This is another way tha
words get changed...
AND EXPLAINS WHY...

Earlier that day, soon after they had landed safely in Blackbank Wood, Grandad Grott had announced:

First of all we must unpick our cat-bugs.

Gribble and the troop unpacked their kit-bags.

Then they

making sure that their tont pigs were set at 45 degrees,

and knocked in firmly with a widden mullet.

Once the tents were up,
they got themselves settled in
and started to think about food.

By the time Dimbert arrived on the scene the Grobblewockians had scoffed a load of sausages, and were sitting around the 'old camp friar', having a sing song.

They were singing that old scouting favourite:

Now, not only were these alien Scouts not singing what you would call *the proper words*, they were also not singing what you would call *the proper tune.*

The fact was, they *didn't know* the proper tune. So to conceal this fact they each sang *a different tune* that they *didn't know* . . .

VERY LOUDLY.

It was all too much for Dimbert. He screwed up his face and let out . . . an **almighty howl.**

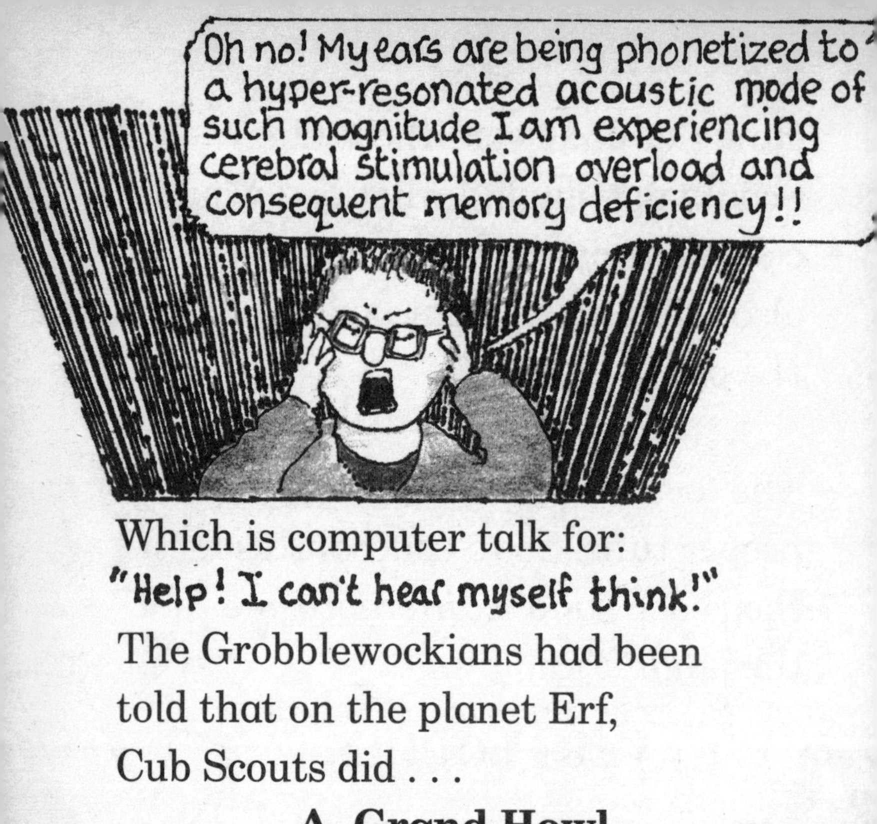

Which is computer talk for:

"Help! I can't hear myself think!"

The Grobblewockians had been told that on the planet Erf, Cub Scouts did . . .

A Grand Howl

. . . but, of course, they'd never actually heard one. Naturally they thought that this was what they were hearing now – and howled back their reply.

I don't know if you've ever been unexpectedly grand-howled at by a troop of alien Scouts, but if so, you probably said what Dimbert said next.
He said:

ARgHeeei!!

He then did what anybody in their right mind would do if an alien monster wearing Scout uniform loomed up to them out of the darkness and said:

He fainted.

Now, when offered a sausage, the average alien being would usually say something like:

'Oh thank you very much'

– and then eat it.

So when Dimbert screamed:

ARgHeeei!!

– and then lay down on the floor, the Grobblewockians were somewhat confused.

said Gribble. He was always keen to show off his first aid skills.

But Grandad Grott said:

So that's what they did.

Next morning the sun rose bright and early.

And it seemed very bright too. He looked through the tent flap and, as if for the first time, saw the outside world.

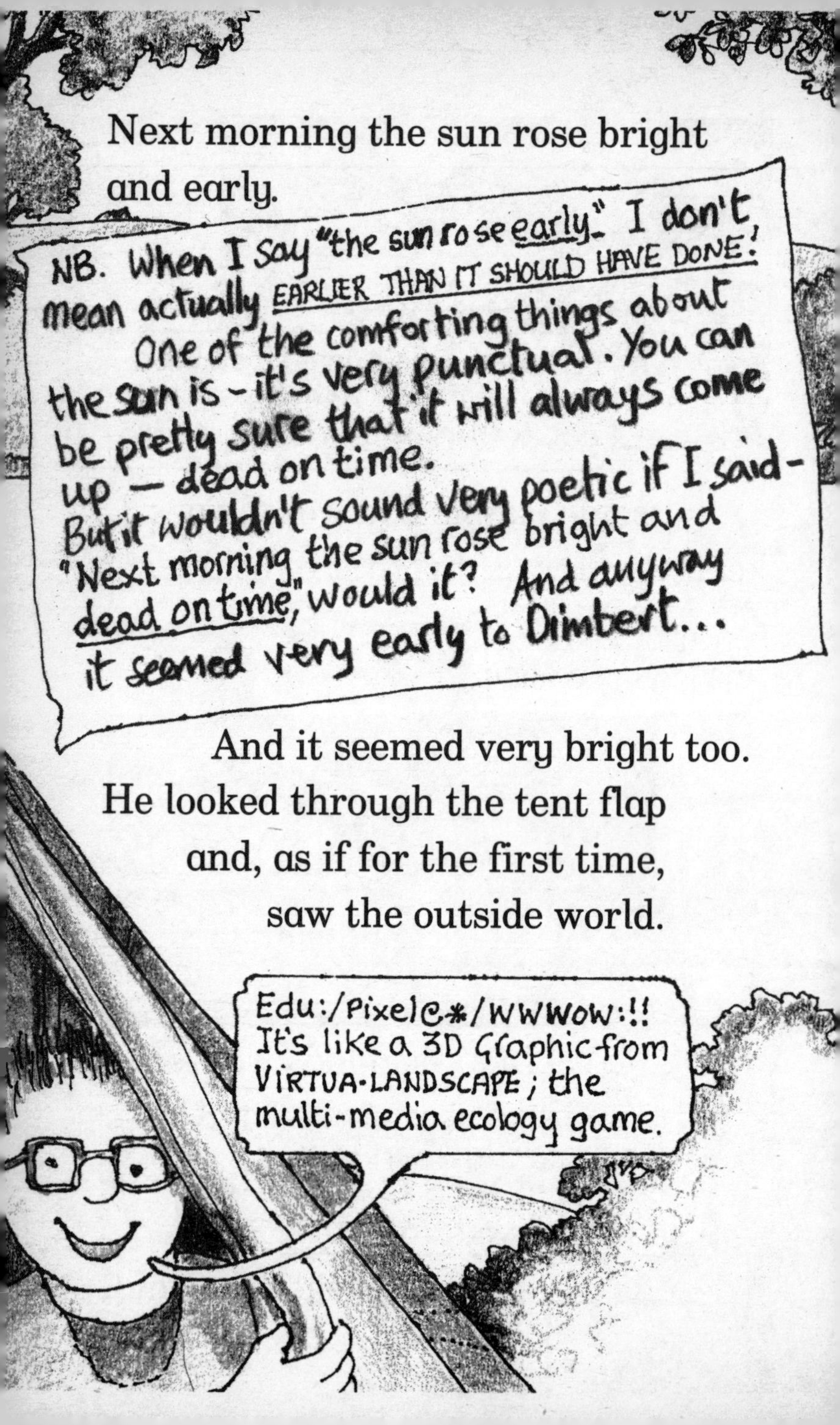

He'd seen the countryside before but only from a distance. It seemed different now that he was in the middle of it.

He was wondering where he was exactly, and how he'd got there when he was suddenly reminded.

What do you think he said next?

Now, if **you** were in a strange wood,
and were suddenly 'Peep Bo'd' by
alien space monsters, would you say:
'Excuse me, I wonder if you'd mind
telling me where I am?'
No. You'd be too scared to speak.
In fact you'd probably be
Alienograhorrywobblified!!
But Dimbert wasn't scared at all.
You see, he spent his days playing
'DOOMBATS' and **'TERRORMAZE'**.
And these alien space monsters
were not half as ugly as . . .

And they seemed quite harmless too.

I expect you're here to take over the world bringing with you weird instruments of **fire, flood** and ultimate destruction.

Mind you, we have brought a blox of mutches.

And a hot-warty bockle.

But actually we're just here for the trees.

'The trees?' enquired Dimbert.
'What about the trees?'

'They don't actually know very much about trees,' thought Dimbert.
True, he didn't know much about trees either.
But he did have his MiCROM/P68 InFotek Pocket-size Computer.
He took it out, loaded a programme entitled

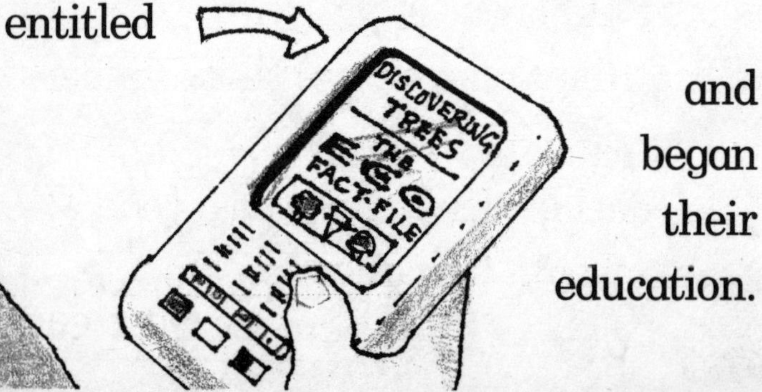

and began their education.

There was something Dimbert didn't understand. If the aliens liked trees, why were they looking so bored?
The reason was simple.
The Grobblewockians knew a few things about trees that Dimbert obviously didn't.
They decided that now was a good time to begin his education. So . . .

They told him about
Tree-huts.
And rope-swings.

And how a tree could be

They taught Dimbert about all sorts of things.
Interesting things, such as . . .

They played
cowboys and aliens,
hide and shriek, throwing stones at a tin can on a stump and jumping up and down on a patch of mud until it went so squishy that you could pretend you were being swallowed up by dangerous quicksands.

And, of course . . .

knot naming.

By the end of the afternoon, Dimbert had come to a realisation.

They were sitting
under a horse-chestnut
tree, wondering what
they could do next,
when Gribble
was struck by a good idea.

Grandad Grott had been listening
to the conversation.
'I remember when I first played
clonkers,' he said. 'It was over
fifty years ago, in this very wood.
And d'you know who it was taught
me to play? Our Great Scouting
Leader; Garry Wimbush.
I wonder where he is now?'
'I know where he is!'
cried Dimbert.

And they did.

And there was a joyous reunion.

And that's how in the year 2052
Dimbert Wimbush will learn the
meaning of friendship, and discover
the wonders of

THE GREAT OUTDOORS

He will still use his computer to help
him with his homework, of course,
and he'll play games on it too.
But not all the time.
On sunny days and Saturdays,
and on misty, moisty autumn days
he will go out into the real world
of fields and woodland, back streets
and parks, and play games *with
other children*, real games which
they **make up themselves.**
And in the evening, snuggled up
in his bed, tired after a boisterous
day, he will think back with pride to
the day that he took part in . . .

. . . the first ever . . .

THE END